Star Party

Originated by Polly Dunbar

WALKER BOOKS
AND SUBSIDIARIES
LONDON · BOSTON · SYDNEY · AUCKLAND

for Nieve, love Polly

Tilly and her friends were putting up tents.
They were going to sleep out in the garden.

"I'm so excited!" said Hector.

"This is going to be fun," said Tilly.

"I love camping out,"
said Tilly.

"It's like being on holiday!" said Doodle.

Everyone got cosy in their sleeping bags.

Tiptoe wasn't ready to go to sleep.
He saw a beautiful blue star
in the sky. It looked lonely.
Tiptoe waved at the blue star.

The star twinkled back!
Tiptoe wanted to play with the blue star.

"Let's ask the star to come down and play," said Tumpty.

"Would you like to come and play?" called Doodle.

The star didn't answer.

Then everyone called.
But still the star didn't answer.

Then Tilly had an idea.

Everyone cut out star shapes
so they could dress up as stars.

"These will make the blue star feel at home," said Tilly.

"Mr Blue Star," said Tilly,
"please come and play with us down here!"

The friends thought food might help,
so they made a twinkly midnight snack.

"Bitey, bitey!"
said Doodle.

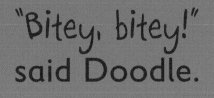

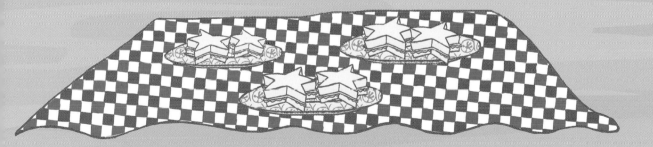

Tiptoe tried to reach the star
wearing Pru's tall shoes.

That didn't work.

Then Tiptoe tried jumping
on the trampoline.

"We need something to blast us into the sky,"
said Tumpty.

"We need a spaceship!"
said Tilly.

A spaceship was just what they needed!

10, 9, 8, 7, 6, 5, 4, 3, 2, 1

BLAST OFF!

They flew for miles and miles and miles.

"The blue star isn't getting any closer," said Doodle.

"It's true," said Tilly.
"The stars may seem close,
but they are a very
long way away."

Tilly and her friends couldn't reach the star.

"But look," said Doodle, "there's another star."

"And another!" said Pru. "And there's the moon."

Tiptoe was happy to see
that the blue star wasn't alone.
And he knew he would see it
again tomorrow night.

And the night after that.

First published 2013 by Walker Books Ltd, 87 Vauxhall Walk, London SE11 5HJ

2 4 6 8 10 9 7 5 3 1

© 2012 JAM Media and Walker Productions
Based on the animated series TILLY AND FRIENDS, developed and produced by Walker Productions and JAM Media
from the Walker Books 'Tilly and Friends' by Polly Dunbar. Licensed by Walker Productions Ltd.

This book has been typeset in Gill Sans and Boopee.

Printed in China

British Library Cataloguing in Publication Data:
a catalogue record for this book is available from the British Library

ISBN 978-1-4063-4832-3

www.walker.co.uk

See you again soon!